G70

PROJECTS ABOUT
The Woodland Indians

David C. King

mc Marshall Cavendish
Benchmark
New York

Marshall Cavendish Benchmark
99 White Plains Road
Tarrytown, NY 10591-9001

Library of Congress Catlaoging-in-Publication Data
King, David C.
Projects about the Woodland Indians / by David C. King
p. cm.—(Hands-on history)
Summary:"Includes Social Studies projects taken from the American Indians of the Eastern Woodlands"--Provided by publisher.
Includes bibliographical references and index.
ISBN 0-7614-1979-9
1. Indians of North America—East (U.S.)—History—Juvenile literature. 2. Indians of North America—East (U.S.)—Social life and customs—Juvenile
literature. I. Title. II. Series.

E78.E2K55 2005
973.04'97074—dc22
2004027456

Illustrations by Rodica Prato

Title page: Portrait of a young Seminole prince

Photo research by Joan Miesel
Photo credits: *Alamy*: Stock Montage, Inc., 8. *Corbis*: Bowers Museum of Cultural Art, 15. *Getty Images*: Hulton Archive, 1. *Marilyn "Angel" Wynn/Na-
tivestock.com*: 20, 23, 26. *North Wind Picture Archives*: 4, 7, 18, 32; Jeff Greenberg, 34.

Printed in China

1 3 5 6 4 2

Contents

Many Woodland Indians built canoes from birch bark.

1
Introduction

Imagine traveling back four hundred years, long before there was a country called the United States of America. You see land covered with forest—forests so thick that in many places the sunlight cannot reach the ground. Women and children are tending crops of corn, squash, and beans, while smaller children fill baskets with wild berries. The men and older boys are nowhere to be seen. They have gone into the forest to hunt with bows and arrows for deer or smaller game like rabbits and wild turkeys.

The Indians of the Eastern Woodlands lived this way for hundreds of years before the Europeans arrived. In the 1600s, people from England and other parts of Europe came to the Atlantic coast of North America. Over the next two hundred years, more and more people came and settled. These settlers pushed into the lands of the Woodland Indians, forcing most of them to move west.

In this book, you will meet people of different tribes and nations, including the Iroquois, Algonquians, Cherokee, and Seminole. You won't just read about Native-American ways of life, you'll learn about their culture by making a model of an Iroquois longhouse, an Algonquian ceremonial drum and drumstick, and dry fruit as the Cherokee did.

Enjoy your travels. As the Algonquian tribes say, *Aupadush shawaindaugoozzeyun,* which means "May good luck attend you." (In Indian languages, pronounce each letter and syllable just the way it looks.)

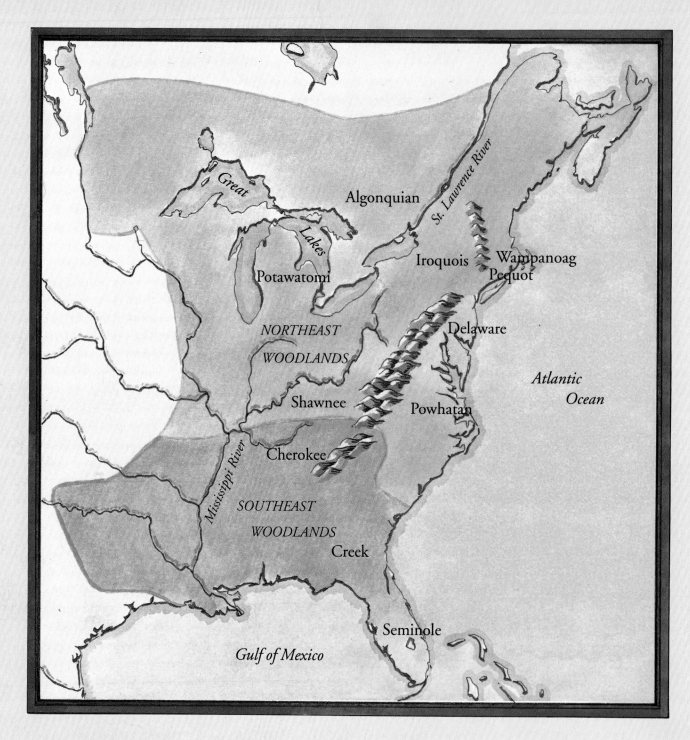

Great Lakes

Algonquian

St. Lawrence River

Iroquois

Wampanoag
Pequot

Potawatomi

NORTHEAST

WOODLANDS

Delaware

Atlantic
Ocean

Shawnee

Powhatan

Mississippi River

Cherokee

SOUTHEAST

WOODLANDS

Creek

Seminole

Gulf of Mexico

This map shows the areas where the Northeast and Southeast Woodland Indians lived. Homelands of the tribes mentioned in this book are also shown.

Native Americans lived on Manhattan Island for thousands of years before European settlers arrived.

Iroquois villages varied in size, from just a few to over a hundred longhouses. Several families shared each longhouse.

2

The Iroquois

The tribes of the Iroquois Nation called themselves *Haudenosaunee*, which means "the people of the longhouse." Their long-houses were made of wood. Heavy tree limbs formed a frame that was then covered with bark "tiles," usually from elm or ash trees. The houses really were long, some were nearly as long as football fields. Longhouses could hold as many as a dozen families.

The Iroquois were strong, especially when all the tribes were united. In the 1600s and 1700s, they resisted when settlers tried to take their lands. Around 1800 the Iroquois decided to make peace with the settlers. Today some Iroquois live on reservations—land set aside for them by the United States government—within New York State. Many others have chosen to live in cities and suburbs.

Model Longhouse

Imagine it is the year 1590. An Iroquois boy named Jis ko-ko, which means "robin," shows you through his family's longhouse. "See the cooking fires in the center?" he asks. "Each family shares a fire with the family on the opposite side. I'm making a model of our longhouse. Come and help me."

Along the walls, there are shelves for sleeping and for storage, like modern bunk beds. Jis ko-ko takes a model longhouse from its shelf. "It's beautiful," you say, "but where are the windows?"

"Windows?" he repeats. "What are windows?"

Longhouses had no windows, only a door at each end and three or four holes in the roof to let smoke from cooking and warming fires escape.

You will need:

- shoe box
- pencil
- sharp knife
- scissors
- 4 or 5 pieces of thin flexible wire, available at hardware and craft stores
- stapler
- 2 sheets of brown or tan crepe paper or tissue paper
- white glue or transparent tape
- 2 sheets of brown or gray construction paper
- 8-12 straight twigs, each about 6 inches long

1. Discard the shoe-box top. On one end of the box, draw a doorway. With an adult's help, cut out the opening with a sharp knife.

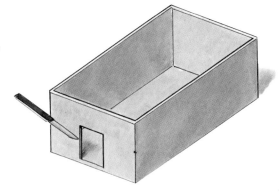

2. To make supports for the rounded roof, measure a piece of wire long enough to reach from the bottom of the box, up the side, then across the top in a curve, and down the other side, as shown. Cut five pieces of wire this length.

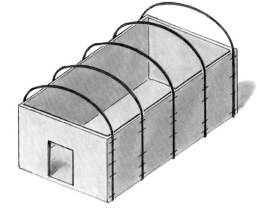

3. Staple the wires to the outside of the box. The first and last wires should be close to the box ends.

4. To make the sides of the box look as if they're covered with bark, cut pieces of crepe paper or tissue paper 6 or 7 inches long and about 1½ inches wide. Starting at the bottom, place a piece of paper lengthwise along one of the long sides squeezing a little glue along the top edge of the strip and pressing it against the box. Overlap the strips a little until all sides are covered.

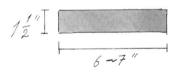

$1\frac{1}{2}''$

$6 \sim 7''$

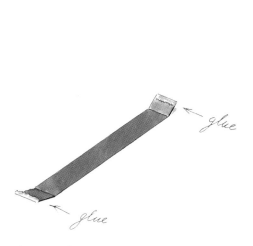

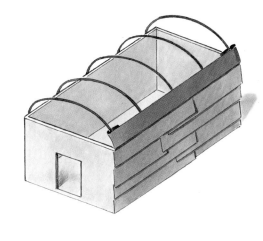

5. Make the roof strips out of the brown or gray construction paper. Measure the length of the shoe box. Cut construction-paper strips this length plus 2 inches, and about 1½ inches wide. Lay a strip lengthwise near the edge of the roof. Fold the ends of the paper strip over and around the end wires. Staple or glue them in place. Repeat until the whole roof is on. Once the glue is dry, cut two smoke holes in the roof with the knife.

6. Glue four to six twigs, standing upright, along the sides of the house as shown.

7. You can make a more elaborate setting for your longhouse by placing it on a large piece of sturdy card-board or thin plywood. Add gravel, stones, bits of dried moss (available at a florist shop or craft store), or any-thing that resembles the Iroquois homeland.

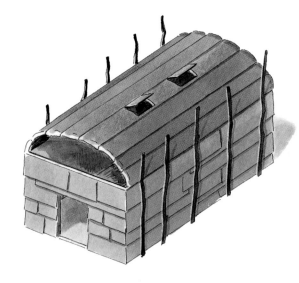

The Basket Game

It is early evening in an Iroquois village. The village is located on a bluff overlooking a long, narrow lake. Six men are sitting in a circle, cross-legged. They shout and chant as they take turns bouncing a basket firmly against the ground, causing some flat stones in the basket to bounce into the air before settling back into the basket.

Jis ko-ko explains: "They are playing a game called the Basket Game or Basket Gamble. All the tribes play it." He tells you that the game could continue all night. Nearly all the tribes love games of chance, and they enjoy gambling. "Sometimes," he says, "they will bet something valuable, even a favorite pony. Come into the longhouse and I'll show you how to play."

You will need:

- piece of stiff cardboard, like the back of a writing pad
- 50-cent piece; or a round, flat object of similar size
- pencil
- red and blue felt-tip pens
- scissors
- small basket or wooden bowl
- 2 or more players
- 40 or more toothpicks, plain or colored, as counting sticks

1. On the cardboard, trace around the fifty-cent piece with the pencil to make six playing pieces.

2. Use the felt-tip pens to make a design on only one side of each piece. The design can be anything you want, and all six can be different or the same.

3. Cut out the playing pieces with the scissors.

4. Sit on the floor across from the other player, or in a circle if there are more than two players. If more than three people play, form teams.

5. Place the game pieces in the basket, and pile the counting sticks on one side.

6. To play, hold the basket with one hand and lightly toss the pieces into the air, then catch them in the basket. Native Americans play the game by holding the basket with both hands and slapping it on the ground, making the game pieces jump.

7. Game pieces that land with the design side up count as one point each. After a player has tossed the pieces, he or she counts the score and takes that many counting sticks from the pile. The second player then does the same. When all the counting sticks are gone, players (or teams) count up their sticks. Whoever has the most is the winner.

False-Face Mask

The year is 1740. A sick girl has been placed on a mat in front of a longhouse. As family and friends gather around, a man dances in front of the girl. He is chanting and wears a strange mask with a scary face.

The Iroquois people believed that illness was caused by evil spirits. These spirits were heads without bodies, who lived in the forest and spread sickness. A special healer, or medicine man, tried to trick the evil ones with the help of the mask, called a false-face mask. The healer would carve the mask into the bark of a living tree. Once he had carved the horrible face, he cut the mask from the tree. Then, the medicine man would dance and chant while wearing the mask. This was believed to confuse or frighten the spirit, who would flee. These special healers were members of a group called the False-Face Society.

Masks made in the morning were painted red; if made later in the day, black was used. But it was quite common to use both colors on a mask.

A traditional wooden mask.

You will need:

- tape measure
- pencil
- large piece of flexible cardboard, about 10 by 14 inches
- scissors
- red and black markers or pens

- a 1-hole punch
- short pieces of yarn, about 5 inches long, in different colors
- ¾ inch wide elastic
- stapler, optional

1. Use a tape measure to measure your face from the top of your forehead to your chin. Then measure from ear to ear. With the pencil, make a rectangle with these measurements on the cardboard. Cut out the cardboard rectangle with the scissors and round off the corners, making a shape like the one in the illustration.

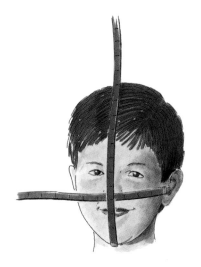

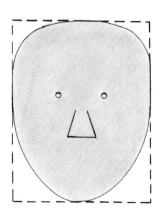

2. Cut out small round holes for your eyes. Don't wear the mask while doing this. Cut a flap for your nose like the one in the drawing. Leave the top of the nose flap attached to the mask.

3. Use red and black markers or pens to make circles around the eye holes. Also draw some designs on the forehead and the nose flap. Draw a large mouth.

4. Use the hole punch to make eight or ten holes along the top edge. Tie the yarn through these holes for the hair.

5. Measure a piece of elastic to stretch around your head from one side of the mask to the other. Punch a hole in the mask where the mask will touch each of your ears. Pull one end of the elastic through one of these holes and tie it as shown. Repeat with the other hole. You may prefer to staple each end of the elastic to the back of the mask. Be sure you are not wearing the mask while stapling.

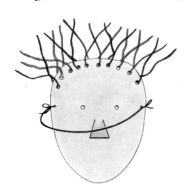

Wigwams were the traditional homes of the Algonquian tribes. These dwellings could easily be built in one day.

3
The Algonquians

While the tribes of the Iroquois Confederation were united and lived near each other, the Algonquian tribes were scattered throughout the Eastern Woodlands. More than fifty tribes were spread from the Atlantic coast in the east to the Great Lakes in the west. The only thing uniting them was their language, called Algonquian.

In 1609, when English colonists first landed in present-day Virginia, they were met by an Algonquian tribe known as Powhatans. At first, the Powhatans helped the colonists, showing them how to plant foods that were unknown in Europe like corn, beans, and squash. Farther north, in what is now Massachusetts, other colonists established a colony at Plymouth in 1620. They, too, were helped by Algonquian tribes—the Pequots and Wampanoag.

By the 1800s, more than three million people from Europe and Africa had settled along the Atlantic coast. Most Algonquian tribes were forced to move west.

Drum

The year is 1780, and the men in a village of the Delaware tribe are preparing for a hunt. The evening before they leave, a ceremony is held around a large fire. The women chant special songs and the men dance or create the rhythm for the dance with drums and rattles.

A Native American storyteller sings and drums traditional songs.

"Music is how we talk to the spirits," a Delaware girl explains. "The hunters make magical animal music, asking for a successful hunt. We also have special songs for planting crops and for harvesting them. When there is a birth, or a death, or a marriage, or any other special occasion, it is time for singing."

1. Ask an adult to help you use the knife to cut the top part off one jug and the bottom parts off both jugs, as shown. The piece that has no top or bottom is called the drumshell.

2. Use markers to draw designs on the outside of the drumshell.

3. Punch holes around the two bottom pieces, spacing the holes about 1¼ inches apart. Make sure you punch the same number of holes on each bottom piece.

4. Place these pieces on the top and bottom of the drumshell.

5. Pull the twine through one of the holes in the bottom piece. Pull all the twine, except for 4 inches, through the hole. Lace the twine up over the outside of the drumshell and through a hole in the top piece, directly above where you started. Pull all the twine through, pass the twine over the out-side of the drumshell, and move on to the next bottom hole. Continue until you've reached the last hole. Pull the twine tight and tie the two ends together. Trim off any excess twine.

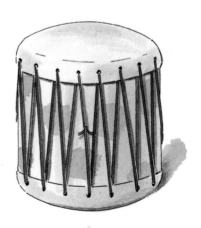

6. Use the straight branch for a drumstick.

Turtle-Shell Rattle

The year is 2004, and you are at a powwow of several Woodland tribes near the Ohio River. Members of the Shawnee nation are performing a ritual dance. The rhythm is provided by drums and rattles. An eleven-year-old Shawnee girl shows you a rattle that looks like a turtle.

"It *is* a turtle shell," the girl explains. "We make rattles out of other things, too, like gourds. But the turtle is special. You see, the people believe that the whole world rides on the back of a great turtle."

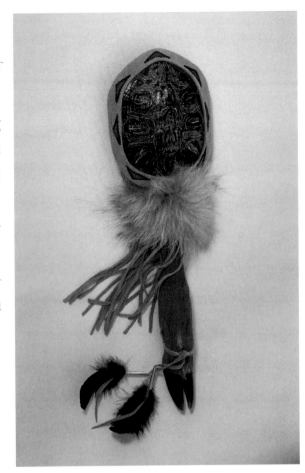

This rattle was made with a turtle shell and a deer hoof.

You will need:

- 2 small, white heavy-duty paper plates, 6-inch size
- pencil
- tempera paints, brown or dark green
- small paintbrush
- stapler
- ¼-½ cup dried beans

1. With a pencil, draw a design on the back of each paper plate that looks like a turtle's shell.

2. Paint the design with brown or dark green paint.

3. Once the paint is dry, have the front of the plates facing each other, then staple the edges together as shown. Leave about 1 inch between staples. Leave an opening of 2 or 3 inches unstapled. Pour the dried beans in through that opening, then staple the opening closed.

beans

4. Use the rattle and the drum together to go along with your own dance rhythms.

Ground Nut Cakes

It is autumn of the year 1828. A group of children are scurrying beneath the trees gathering nuts. A young boy tells you that one winter the people of his tribe, the Potawatomi, had nothing to eat but nuts. "Another tribe had forced us to leave our home," he tells you. "We had to find a new place to live, and we did not even have time to harvest our corn and squash. Would you like to try a nut cake?"

You will need:

- 2 cups raw nuts (any kind), without shells and unsalted
- cookie sheet
- wooden spoon
- 2 potholders
- food processor or grinder
- mixing bowl
- 1 teaspoon vanilla
- ½ cup maple syrup
- ½ cup flour
- corn-oil spray (like Pam)

Makes 15-20 cakes

1. Ask an adult to help. Wash your hands.
2. Set the oven to 300 degrees Fahrenheit. Spread the nuts on a cookie sheet in a single layer. Bake the nuts, stirring often, about fifteen to twenty minutes, until they are roasted. Be careful not to let them burn. Remove the cookie sheet from the oven using pot holders. Set aside until cool.
3. Set the oven to 350 degrees Farhenheit.
4. Grind the nuts in a food processor or grinder until they look like coarse sand.
5. Place the ground nuts in a mixing bowl. Add the vanilla and maple syrup.
6. Gradually stir in the flour to make dough. Add a little at a time. You may find it easier to mix the dough with your fingers. Form the dough into round patties 3 inches across.
7. Spray the cookie sheet with the cooking spray. Place the nut cakes on the sheet about 2 inches apart.
8. Bake at 350 degrees Fahrenheit for five to ten minutes until the nut cakes are firm and lightly browned. Remove the cookie sheet from the oven with potholders. Serve your nut cakes warm.

Before the Europeans arrived, Cherokee women wore doeskin dresses.

4

The Cherokee

In the late 1700s and early 1800s, the people of the Cherokee Nation hoped to live at peace with the growing numbers of white settlers. Their solution was to try to live the way white Americans lived. The Cherokee kept their own language and customs, but they built houses, schools, and roads like European Americans.

A great Cherokee chief named Sequoya helped their cause by creating a written alphabet for the Cherokee language. Sequoya's alphabet had eighty-five symbols or letters, each representing a syllable or sound in Cherokee. The written language worked very well, and thousands of Cherokee learned it. There was even a Cherokee newspaper. Many white Americans were impressed, and the Cherokee became known as one of the "Five Civilized Tribes."

But the Cherokee were not able to hold back the land-hungry settlers. In 1830, President Andrew Jackson ordered the army to move all the eastern tribes to lands west of the Mississippi River in present-day Oklahoma. Over the next few years, the Cherokee sadly followed what they called the Trail of Tears and began a new life in the Indian Territory.

Dried Fruit and Fruit Leather

It is summertime in 1820. The women and children of a Cherokee village are gathering berries. A young girl explains, "We gather the berries in baskets that we weave out of thin strips of wood. We take the fruit home and dry it in the sun. That way we can have fruit even in the winter."

Here are recipes for two different ways of preserving fruit. Try the sun-drying method if you can. If the weather doesn't cooperate, make the fruit leather instead. Both are delicious.

Dried Fruit
You will need:

- 3 or 4 kinds of fresh fruit; berries, peaches, pears, and plums work well
- table knife or paring knife
- 1 or 2 cookie sheets with sides, or jelly roll pans
- cheesecloth
- 4-6 clothespins
- sunlight and outdoor temperature of at least 70 degrees Fahrenheit
- glass or plastic container with lid

1. Wash the fruit. Cut larger fruits into bite-sized pieces with the knife. Leave the skin on, but throw away the pits and large seeds. Remember to ask an adult to help with sharp knives.

2. Spread the fruit on the cookie sheet(s) and cover it with a single layer of cheesecloth.

3. Use clothespins to hold the cheesecloth in place, as shown. Keep the cloth from touching the fruit as much as possible.

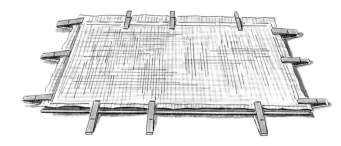

4. Place the fruit outdoors in the sun. A picnic table is ideal. Leave the fruit in the sun all day and bring it in when the sun goes down. Repeat for two or three days.

5. The fruit will become leathery. Don't let it become crisp.

6. Store the fruit in a plastic or glass container with a tight lid. It will keep for several weeks.

Fruit Leather
You will need:

- table knife or paring knife
- 3 or 4 kinds of fruit, about 2 cups
- blender
- cookie sheet
- plastic wrap
- wooden mixing spoon
- glass or plastic container with cover

1. Cut the fruit into pieces, as for sun-dried fruit.

2. With an adult's help, place the fruit in a blender and press *Pulse* for fifteen seconds.

3. Line a cookie sheet with plastic wrap.

4. Pour the fruit mixture onto the plastic wrap. Use the spoon to spread the fruit evenly.

5. Store the cookie sheet in a warm place to dry for about twenty-four hours. Peel off some of the fruit to sample it, then roll up the rest in its plastic wrap and store it in a container with a lid. The fruit leather will keep for weeks.

Toss-and-Catch Game

The year is 1985, and an important celebration is being held in the Great Smoky Mountains of North Carolina. A young man is telling about the celebration. "In 1838," he says, "when our ancestors were forced to move west to Oklahoma on the Trail of Tears, some of our people hid in these mountains and the army could not find them. This year a torch from the campfire in Oklahoma was carried here and added to our campfire. That means the two parts of the Cherokee nation are united again."

To celebrate, a great feast has been prepared, dances are performed, and games are played. The game of Toss and Catch is one of the most popular. "It helps build your skill in catching a ball on a stick," the young man says, "just like lacrosse."

You will need:

- ruler
- pencil
- piece of stiff cardboard, at least 6 by 6 inches
- scissors
- white glue
- a 1-hole punch
- thin dowel, about 12 inches long
- string, 24-26 inches long

1. Use the ruler and pencil to draw a triangle, with all sides about 3 inches long, on the cardboard. Cut out the triangles. Trace that triangle on the cardboard and cut it out.

2. Glue one triangle on top of the other. (The Native Americans used pieces of bone, so your double cardboard also will make a sturdy game piece.)

3. Use the hole punch to make a hole near the center of the triangle. Push the dowel through the hole. Wiggle the dowel to make the hole a bit larger. Then take the triangle off the dowel.

4. Make a small hole near the edge of the game piece and tie one end of the string to it, as shown.

5. Tie the other end tightly to the dowel about 3 inches from the end of the dowel.

6. To play the Toss-and-Catch Game, hold the stick in one hand. Hold the dowel end farthest from the string. Toss the triangle target in the air with the other hand. The goal is to catch the target by having the dowel go through the hole in the center.

7. Each player has three tosses. Score one point for each catch.

8. If the game seems too difficult, you can make two more holes in the target and make them a little larger.

In the 1800s, the Seminole invented dwellings called *chickees*. These shelters made it easier to move to different camps. The Seminole traveled from place to place as they were forced from their lands by U. S. troops.

5

The Seminole

The Seminole were originally part of the Creek Nation, but the advance of white settlers onto their lands forced them to flee to Florida in the 1700s. They were joined there by many Africans who were trying to escape from slavery. The word *Seminole* means "Runaway."

In the 1830s and 1840s, the United States army fought a long war against the Seminole to force them to move west to Indian Territory. The Seminole fought back and moved deep into the swamplands of the Florida Everglades. Although most Seminole finally surrendered and resettled in modern-day Oklahoma, small bands remained defiant. Their descendants continue to live in the Everglades today.

Dolls for sale at a Seminole craft festival.

Corncob Doll

The year is 1920. An elderly Seminole woman is showing her granddaughter how to create a dress for the doll that the old woman made out of a corncob. "When I was a young girl," she explains, "we made dolls out of anything we could find—sticks, rocks, or plants. For your doll, we'll use strips of cloth to make a skirt and a jacket."

You will need:

- 1 ear of corn, fresh or frozen
- table knife
- black marker or felt-tip pen
- ruler or tape measure
- 10-12 scraps of yarn, each 4 or 5 inches long, for the hair

- scissors
- white glue
- 2 pieces of fabric, each about 4 by 8 inches (felt works well)
- 2 or 3 scraps narrow ribbon; to decorate clothes

1. With an adult's help, scrape the kernels off the corn with a table knife. Let the cob dry for a few days.

2. Use black marker or pen to draw eyes, a nose, and a mouth on the rounded end of the cob.

3. Measure the yarn scraps with the ruler or tape measure. Mark them all at the same length—either 4 or 5 inches. Cut them with the scissors.

4. Place a thin line of glue along where the part in the doll's hair would be. Press half of the ends of the yarn strands into the glue, so that the yarn-hair falls down one side of the head. Repeat on the other side of the head with the rest of the yarn.

5. Wrap one rectangle of fabric around the lower half of the doll to form a skirt. Keep the top edge of the cloth tight around the cob. Let the lower edge of the cloth be looser, as shown. At the back of the skirt, put glue along one edge of the cloth that goes up and down. Overlap the other up-and-down edge, and press it onto the glue. Be sure to pull tightly enough so the skirt stays on the doll.

6. Wrap the second rectangle of fabric around the upper part of the doll, in the same way, to form a jacket. Glue as you did the skirt.

7. Cut two small "hands" out of the remaining fabric and glue them to the inside edge of the jacket, as shown.

8. Glue two or three pieces of narrow ribbon around the jacket and the skirt. Use colors that contrast with the skirt and jacket colors.

Woodland Pouch

It is 1830. A Seminole boy is cutting a piece of deerskin to make a pouch. Since Native Americans did not have pockets in their clothing, all of the tribes made different sized bags and pouches. Smaller pouches were used to carry small tools, objects to use in ceremonies, or flints to use for starting a fire. Each tribe had its own designs for decorations. Iroquois used flower designs, while the Seminoles preferred zigzag lines and contrasting colors.

You will need:

- pencil
- piece of paper, at least 10 by 15 inches
- piece of tan felt or chamois, about 8 by 10 inches. Note: chamois cloth is available at hardware stores
- scissors
- box of straight pins
- fabric glue, or, for a more long-lasting pouch, use needle and thread
- braid trim, or substitute thin ribbon or yarn

1. With the pencil, copy the pattern pieces (A and B) onto the paper. Cut out the patterns.

A

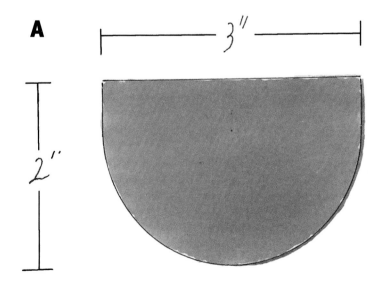

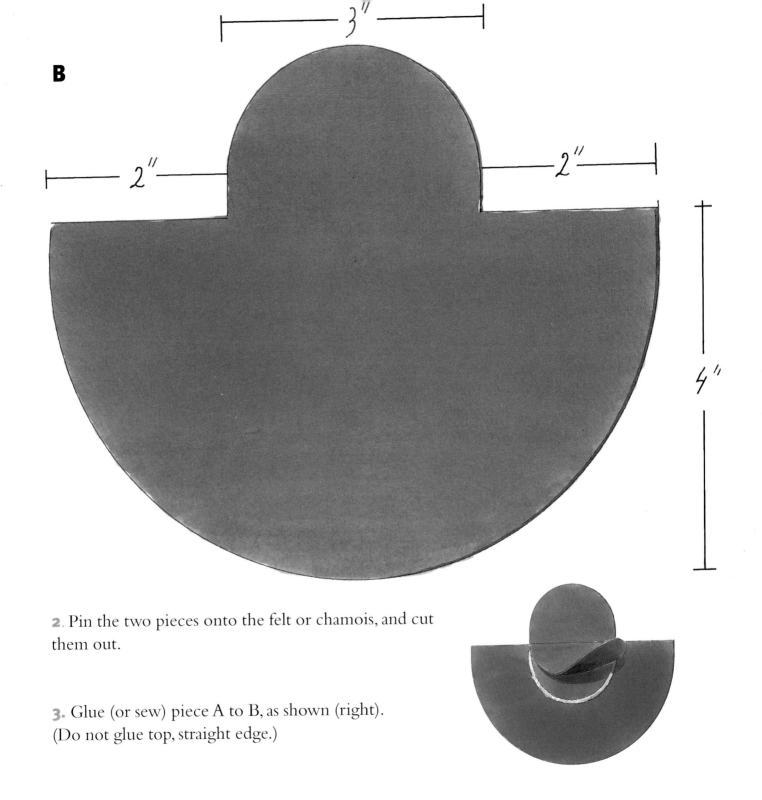

B

3"

2"

2"

4"

2. Pin the two pieces onto the felt or chamois, and cut them out.

3. Glue (or sew) piece A to B, as shown (right). (Do not glue top, straight edge.)

4. Draw a zigzag design onto piece A. Glue braid trim over the design.

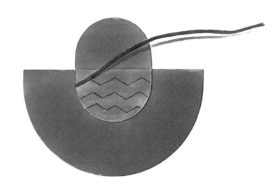

5. Fold down the top of piece B to form a flap over the pocket. Draw the zigzag design on the flap. Glue braid trim onto the design, as in step 4.

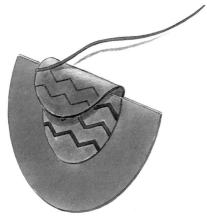

6. With scissors, cut fringes, about ¾ inch deep, all the way around the bottom, as shown.

Glossary

Algonquian: The common language spoken by dozens of Native American tribes, including the Delaware, Pequot, Powhatan, Potawatomi, Shawnee, and Wampanoag.

chamois: A cotton fabric made to imitate chamois leather. Available at hardware and auto parts stores, it is often used for drying off cars after washing.

Five Civilized Tribes: A name given to the five major tribes of the southeastern United States: the Cherokee, Chickasaw, Choctaw, Muskogee (Creeks), and Seminoles. Europeans arriving to the Woodland regions were impressed by these groups' systems of government and education.

medicine man: In Native American culture, a person who uses magic to cure illness and keep away evil spirits.

reservations: Land set aside by the U.S. government for Native American tribes or nations.

Trail of Tears: In 1838, more than 15,000 Cherokee were forced to walk 700 miles from their homeland to Indian territory in Oklahoma.

Find Out More

Books

Haslam, Andrew. *North American Indians*. Chicago: World Book, 1997.

Murdoch, David. *North American Indians*. New York: Alfred A. Knopf and the American Museum of Natural History, 1995.

Sita, Lisa. *Indians of the Northeast: Traditions, History, Legends, and Life*. Philadelphia: Running Press, 1997.

Web Sites:

The American Indian Library Association Web Page
www.nativeculture.com/indians.html

The Seminole Tribe of Florida
www.seminoletribe.com/

History of the Cherokee
www.cherokeehistory.com

Learn About Native Americans
www.ahsd25.k12.il.us/Curriculum%20Info/NativeAmericans/index.html

Metric Conversion Chart

You can use the chart below to convert from U. S. measurements to the metric system.

Weight
1 ounce = 28 grams
½ pound (8 ounces) = 227 grams
1 pound = .45 kilogram
2.2 pounds = 1 kilogram

Liquid volume
1 teaspoon = 5 milliliters
1 tablespoon = 15 milliliters
1 fluid ounce = 30 milliliters
1 cup = 240 milliliters (.24 liter)
1 pint = 480 milliliters (.48 liter)
1 quart = .95 liter

Length
¼ inch = .6 centimeter
½ inch = 1.27 centimeters
1 inch = 2.54 centimeters

Temperature
100°F = 40°C
110°F = 45°C
350°F = 180°C
375°F = 190°C
400°F = 200°C
425°F = 220°C
450°F = 235°C

About the Author

David C. King is an award-winning author who has written more than forty books for children and young adults, including *The Navajo* and *The Sioux* in the Marshall Cavendish First Americans series. He and his wife, Sharon, live in the Berkshires at the junction of New York, Massachusetts, and Connecticut. Their travels have taken them through most of the United States.

Index

Page numbers in **boldface** are illustrations.